The Revelations of (X)
Cross Fiction Series

THE VERSES OF INFINITY

By (Grace) Daniel Cornelius
Ruiter aka. Dragonfly

The Verses Of Infinity

tellwell

Tellwell Talent
www.tellwell.ca

ISBN
978-0-2288-6356-4 (Hardcover)
978-0-2288-6355-7 (Paperback)

ϖ (Pi) is 3x3 = and x5 is ∞ (Infinity)!

There is a warm ball of energy in front of me;
It is my happiness, and I'm trying to absorb it back in.
It is the Earth's …GAIA's happiness, and there is nothing
more precious …or priceless …to quench my will and desire.

To protect her is my only "1 TRUE CALLING!"
And all true beings, dead and living.

"I suffer for you all, by absorbing your pain,"
And now I carry imprisoned in me 3 brothers of taint & slain.
To gorge upon the Darkness, and thrust it again,
…Into the light, to be cleansed
forevermore …Never to remain!

- So Shall it Be.

A TALE OF LÀSCERÍTE:
The Centre of the Universes

There's a place in the unknown of emptiness appetite which I know deep down exists even though never physically witnessed,

But in the *Cosmos* among the things which we are yet untempted by, we ignore the universal truths of creation and aim instead but to suppress.

Of The People of Free Thought and of LIFE itself, no one is to know what threats abound our simple tiny meagre realities,

And this Universal Centre unknown to mankind hath sent forth a 3rd time, reckoning success to cleanse us of our false power frailties.

1st of all there came the Síthe, bringing Darkness Lord who did Reign and fall to Lucifer, changing Hell from Kingdom of Ept. *(Reaper Vs Daemon)*

2 stolen kingdoms merged with one another, but its dwellers are not ones who wept. - *(Poseidon & Kronos or Chronos)*

2nd came the Death-Techs after Time Lords sent them to Void, thus losing their material composition,

But in the same time within Earthrealm rhyme, a sole alien man helped Dalek-Humanoid Preposition. *(Virtuoso-X aka The Doctor …Who? ;-)*

3rd now is a threat of the Làsceríte Death, angelic doth seem an Overfiend,

In comparison to this, self-destruction would seem bliss, but we mustn't lose ourselves, or we'll NOT exist again. *(The Grimmace Antifiend Plague)*

Mankind, unwilling, are to be forced into unison to combat this new threat, but as we look a little further, we see similar patterns in our own typical best.

The intentions we held dear to us will be clearly proven burnt, tainted, and lost,

But once we all realise this, we will ALL come forth ready to fight FOR OUR ONE TRUE CAUSE!

...Victory is ETERNAL when fighting for nature, so if it is a THREAT it MUST FALL!

I'm talking of The System! There is NO other way ...Never has been! ...FOR THE BLOOD IS SURE FOR ALL!

Desirae & Anastasia

She starts ever so gently touching the nodes of life,
Letting herself both moan on top mantle
giving sweet relief little with no scythe.
As she moves closer to her ultima of complexion,
she orgasms without fail condemning
...The knife
...Accuracy within intimacy
Evermore with lust combined into compassion inside
...The grace of God! Herself & Herself
Everlasting pleasure ...The foundation of youth.

ENVISIONED WISDOM:
My Eternal Blood!

What is true possession?
Is it the bloodlines of the past?
Are they Ancestors of tradition?
Or something truly dark?

In my experience as the possessed
I see no truth in this
For we still remain ourselves.
No matter who invokes in dis

Order is a perception
As is chaos as well.
Don't be fooled by deception
As the light is more a bell.

The sound of intuition
The feeling overwhelms
And when one feels a God inside
One knows they've just skipped Hell.

- So shall my path be lit.

EYES = Celestial Doorways! (Riddle)

1. I am so old, so ancient & ageless,
2. Yet I am so young.
3. I know of all things, I've witnessed creation,
2. Yet I truly know nothing.
1. I am so far extreme, my aura is magnificent,
2. Yet I still feel so insignificant.

1.2.3.4. So, who are we, and why are we here?

1.2.3.4. ...We are many ...Find yourself to find us all!

1. ...Find The Creator and you will not fall!
4. I am so bold, so brazen,
2. Yet I am so scared.
4. I have no true fear, nor calculation in matters of the heart.
1. Will you walk with me without resentment?
3. Or will you try to hurt me ...Yourself!
4. When will you learn you cannot beat me?
3. Let's leave those trivial uncertainties for ...
1. So do you know who I am? Figured it out yet?!
4. Go look in the mirror; you'll see us reflect!

ANS = I AM, WE ARE YOU!

1. Now can you stop forcing us ...Please?

1.2.3.4. (PAST/PRESENT/FUTURE) – For We Are Real!!!

- AMEN-

<u>**KEY:**</u> 1=Wrath/2=Greed/3=Lust/4=Pride

FORGOTTEN?

In our tunnel of life, which floweth past our eyes,
We almost always had our difficult times,
But now I have no sight, no sense at
all …Nothing now left in me.
This empty place I once endeared, now
seemingly only endured by you …And yet
you were the one who always betrayed!

My purest thoughts can only perceive me as a blinded fool
To the truth, given that our emotions are
the most obvious of instincts.
The more I try to forget your …the less
I'm able to control myself.
Am I a shadow? Was I mistaken? Did you
ever really see us as "meant to be?"
Or have you simply just …

(Originally written for Jodie Pannell)

I AM ...EQUAL TO YOU!

What Am I?
...Who ...Am I?
Where do I come from ...Truly?
What is my purpose? ...Where do I belong?

All these questions ...So freely and easily ...Ponder my
mind ...Acutely, vaguely, sometimes like a hurricane,
sometimes surreal or sublime.
Every little step taken ...closer ...Closer to the truth!
But when I become angry ...I morph, quite the brute.

I Am NOT a monster ...For a monster will destroy...
Everything in its path ...With no successful decoy...
I do feel a little obscure ...Free to stray ...Free to hate!
And then, I'll see through ...That others feel the same.

Now surrounded by ...Humanoid counterparts
An Ex-Daemoness ...Wishes ...To teach me of intimacy
Bonds form which seem unbreakable, but so
desperately wanted ...dearly needed.
A passion will form ...Unstoppable ...And the Trinity cometh
To the beating hearts ...of the seeded!

A journey to share ...Of warm friendships and bliss...
Not before a love ...Cut short ...Thrown into abyss.
A hurt so deep ...Like a heart that is
tearing ...Crushing ...Suffocating,
"Oh God help me breathe."
Nothing left to anger with ...No material will be left in reach.

A light appearing distant ...A glimmer of lost hope...
A voice deep from within its shimmer ..."Son,
please do not mope.
I know you're sad; I know what you need ...But
what lies ahead, I need you to see.
For I have chosen and sent forth you, my son, to guide,
And you never need fear me ...As I'll always be at your side."

My eyes light up ...Joy springing my first human tear...
As I witness Creation such ...Sweet song in my ears...
I know now the secret ...To which I'll endure...
The truth of all being and all that
exists ...all that which is pure.
I know now I Am REAL ...I have been
given a great PURPOSE,
And when Earthrealm is here again ...I
WILL venture back to its surface.

I know what I Am ...Now know what I must be...
I know where I'm from ...My reason is now seen...
I'll wait for you, my love, to hold you once again,
Never fear, my love, for this time has no end.
I know I Am of LIGHT, and you once opposed me,
And when we are united again, we will balance perfectly!

...But you need to be Awakened ...Aware
of this one true thing...
We are all of THE Light ...Let us shine the PATH together...
For Eternity ...For I Am EQUAL TO ALL of you...

- So shall it be.

I DUALLY WED 321 – Spiritually

There is sadness which lingers
In my every waking hour, in my every breath.
It takes me strength of bringer
To hold back this busting flower, not before death.

- YOUR ESSENCE FILLS MY EXISTENCE -

I couldn't bear to be a stranger for another day.
I can't bear to be without you when you're away.
To feel like this forever is not at one's request to sorrow.
I have other plans on the other side ...My
COMPLETE Heart I Shall Follow

IF I DON'T HAVE YOU?

I am merely someone of ultimate perception in morality;
You've turned nearly every wonderful thought into reality.
When we are as 1 we synchronise like
the flow of water, running bold.
You are the one real true feeling who gives me all ...Love.

You are my dream of ultimate completion;
You are in my every wishful truth.
You are gorgeous and beautiful, intelligently charming;
The mysterious ways in which you work
give me motive to pursue.

You are always here, always smiling, through
your eyes and through your heart;
Your quit-wit and generosity show even when hurt.
Your contentment in mind is of great divine comfort;
You, and only you, undress my every
motion, observing ...aware & alert.

I have only little to offer, but my heart
is true, my offer in depth.
I need you in my life ...No, I'm not mistaken, I have no regret.
All I'm really saying is that "I LOVE
YOU" with no sense to rule,
And to my sweet adorable angel, I have
nothing ...If I Don't Have You!

(Originally written for Stacey Wolter)

I'LL LIVE FOR U!!!

Your fate is mine,
...My love is yours.
If you take your life
In vain, you'd be taking my soul.
If it were me
The same, I'd be taking yours too.
To die for you is only natural,
So, stay alive for me now?
...And I'll live just for you!!!

INEVITABLE WEALTH OF WEAKNESS!

The peasants today
Are living in a way
Which most of us wouldn't survive.
If unholy war came
Into disarray
We all know the ones who would thrive.

If you would just lay
With your head upon clay,
You would feel your own presence inside.
And GOD only knows
Why you're full of such sorrow,
Because life is so peaceful and wise.

Your greed is your end,
But you will not bend
For your money is your suicidal grace.
And when you are judged
In your Heaven on love,
What will you say of your place?

SURVIVAL OF THE STRONGEST
...NOT OF WEALTH
STRENGTH ONLY FROM WITHIN THE LIGHT
WILL BE THE ONLY ONE TO SHINE SO BRIGHT!
TO START AFRESH A BRAND-NEW DAY
...AND KEEP THE DARKNESS FAR AWAY!

- So shall it be.

INFINITE GAIA:
Our Mother's Grace!

Mother, I sense your yearning;
I feel deeply your every pain.
Yet you proceed to accept me,
And still, you show me the way.

(Infinitely) Without her we wouldn't be here
Not to be, amongst life and her might.
No life existing to see clear
Her beauty, from the grandest of heights.

Mother, I hear you constantly crying;
I see you falling hard to your knees.
But we already know you're not lying;
Your honesty is as blunt as rock and breeze.

Affluent sensual essence of all-natural creation
Nurturing my every true need.
Humbling my deepest of gratitude,
I live to serve your every heed.

Effervescence of her grace so pure,
Awakening my very first breath.
So, when my life is spent and done with lure,
Into her arms I fall and will not taste …

- So shall she be.

JESUS, O THOU HEART Leo!

You floweth beneath thy breast;
Your song runneth down all rivers.
Your beat within thine heart,
Your harmony slowly tethers.

Your tempest all inviting
To the steeple test of knowing,
Your spectrum of all brightening
To the dimming hark of sowing.

Your seed now planted of evening,
Our waking moments to the future.
Your presence of eternal tendering,
Our purpose a son to now nurture.

He with the knowledge of creation
To be himself, to be of artistic band.
He of miraculous immaculate conception
To lead them to the promised land.

- AMEN -

(Originally written for my son Leo)

KARMA: I Am …Everyone, Everyone is …Me!

If I hurt myself …it will hurt you.
If I hurt you …I hurt myself.
If you hurt me …you hurt yourself.
When we hurt one another, we only hurt ourselves.

If I beat myself …I beat you.
If I beat you …I beat myself.
If you beat me …you'll beat yourself.
When we beat one another, we only beat ourselves.

If I forget myself …I'm forgetting you.
If I forget you …I'm forgetting myself.
If you forget me …you're forgetting yourself.
When we forget one another, we only forget ourselves.

But If I forgive myself …I'm forgiving you.
If I forgive you …I'm forgiving myself.
If you forgive me …you are forgiving yourself.
If we forgive each other, we always forgive ourselves.

And If I were to love myself …I will love you.
If I were to love you …then I will love myself.
If you were to love me …Then you will love yourself.
So, in turn, if we all were to love each other …Platonically
and/or Deeply, then we would all ultimately love
ourselves truly …And all other Life …Without Vanity!

LiFE CODE! (Verse)

Apart from God Almighty, the human mind is the most powerful sign of Mother Earth (GAIA), yet we choose to ignore it.

Our own happiness comes from within ...

It only takes the "right" person to open our hearts and show us our own true inner beauty.

But it can also take the "wrong" person to show you your inner "Daemon of Hatred & Sin!" The Aggressor Beast to bring out your worst colour ...of sadness and deep depression, unwanting to be ...

- Alone ...Nowhere -

The strength within one's freedom of thoughts and emotions gives us the control and the power over what we fear most ...Ourselves!

To stay in self content and to keep all of your mind open in all reasonable optimism ...is to show maturity, to accept things as they are, to advise change without force, thus showing the path ...of Forgiveness! Wanting to be...

- Foreverness ...Clarity -

- eternal grace, honesty, and the pure essence of deeply true love ...

- which can only be felt to be founded, never told nor written, for its scale on paper will always be far away from reality's scale ...

"GOD'S WISH, GOD'S PROMISE ...into Eternal Life"

Look for the things you can create real change to take favour, and the virtue will spread like the gusts of the Autumn Storm in Australia!

Life is Bella!

We go up and we go down,
And life is all around us.
We grow up and we grow down,
And strife becomes a part of us.

We want this and we want that,
In disarray we are delusional.
To be the abyss, to be a big brat,
To be inconsistent is not beautiful.

But we learn and become concerned
As life itself teaches us lessons.
Back to state of mind of the childlike grind,
Somehow, we must lean into confessions.

So, we are and I am
The most original me I can be;
I will imprint all I can
To teach those to go beyond me.

Life is Bella
Life is Bella
Life is Bella ...Life is Beautiful!

Longing

Eyes imprinted on my soul,
thus darkness diminishing,
Wandering the astral planes,
Is that you in infinity?

A smile melts the heart,
taking me to a cloaked place.
The solace undeniably true,
a cloth of satin and white lace.

Mind in state of mesmerisation
as the Goddess connects 2.
Rainbows of joy after a giant storm
reaches out for inner self view.

Your voice is nothing but comfort;
I long for your touch.
Meet me in the Elysium Fields.
A kiss I ask ...not much.

MEMORIES OF BARACK of the 1st Australians!

Long will live the memories
Of the 1st Australians at Coranderrk
In my heart, in my mind, and within my children ...

I Am White, I Am Brown, I Am Black, I Am Sound.
I Am Ethnic, I Am Yellow, I Am Red, I Will Bellow.
I Am Coloured & When I'm Blue I Search
for Things Which Are True.
I am Pean; I'm of Stan; Step on Us, WE WILL NOT Run!

Long will live the memories
Of the 1st Australians at Coranderrk
In my heart, in my mind, and within my children ...

I Stand for All: All of the Sons, All of the
Daughters, And All of the Mothers.
I Stand for All of the Fathers, All of My Brothers,
and All of Our People they tried to slaughter.
You see, our ancestors of The Great Britons Isle they
most turned to Darkness in a "Rum Core" pile.
To put them down, to breed them out, to destroy
their cultures and dreamtimes futile.

Long will live the memories
Of the 1st Australians at Coranderrk
In my heart, in my mind, and within my children ...

I Will Not STOP, I Cannot HEED to a Racist Society of Greed!
Of Vanity, with Envied Hearts ...WE'LL BREAK
Your TREND of Poisoned Darts!
Of Shooting Guns And Great Big Mouths ...WE'LL
Make You SHUT Your EMPTY SHOUTS!!!
Those things have no true statement. EMPTY
are ALL who are COMPLACENT!

Long will live the memories
Of the 1st Australians at Coranderrk.
In my heart, in my mind, and within
my children …HENCEFORTH!
…For a future we will not doubt!

(In Memory of Barack of the 1st Australians)

MY SACRIFICE: (H/J) = Yin & Yang (Heart)

There is a place inside me
That only one else knows.
This heart was falling blindly
But with two hands he arose

Towards a hidden bounty
Which suddenly came clear,
And all the rules around us
Did suddenly appear.

The Rose has now awakened
Slightly angered hearth
And with careful nurtured comfort
Becoming loyal, not of Dark

For a light has shone upon thee.
I have 1 fear to share:
Without both hearts' death on me
I take all their sins to bear

P.S. I'm Bleeding Me …
My Poetry …My Confession

NEVER FALL FAVE NEIN (459) - Queen Creation

Who could begrudge a mother?
The one who gave you first breath,
The one who wiped boogers from ya mouth and nose,
And the one who catches you still in
times you flirt with death.

Who would protect a mother?
The one who protects you now,
The one who freely changed your bottom,
And the one who powdered you up
with a lovely perfumed bow

Who will care for a mother?
The one who ages beautiful grace,
The one who'll need her diapers changed,
Because one day in reality you'll be in her place.

So always show your love for a mother,
For you know not the burden she bears
Of keeping all the important things together,
And teaching you most importantly ...To share.

...I love you, Mum, and faved you,
...And I'll never let you fall **XÖX**

So Long

I have been here since the beginning,
Since the beginning of time.
I am bored and overjoyed at birth of life.
Should I be joyous or sad for death or just whine?

I married a ghost at 14; she waits for me.
In the shadows she lurks
As I do my lightwork, saving all of thee.
Only my son keeps me …It hurts.

I was suicidal once but had not the courage.
They threw me in hospital and said I had issues.
They didn't ask why …I wouldn't age.
They didn't care to look at who I was …In truth.

My youth is endless. If I had beauty
It would be divine and eternal.
My Blood is my soul, it is my serenity.
I age not at all; my love is infernal.

So do I believe in a God? Of course I do.
I also know of a Goddess inside …She is so strong.
I am impenetrable …I will stay true
To the Lord and Lady …I will do no wrong.

"So It Will Be."

The Air I Breathe

With this air I softly whisper
To your heart that I long for.
On this Earth I will prosper,
And to the fire I give all.

To reach the stars I will bend,
But with flow I will not break.
An oath to you I do send
Of all the riches I will not take.

Your life is worth more
Than all wealth in worlds.
I treasure your soul,
Like the sea treasures pearls.

We will tumble on the way,
But will not fall into or stray.
Stand by me and I will say
That I love you every day.

- So Mote It Be.

The Calamity of Reason

The warm calming of her grace
Brings effervescence of Spring's rays.
The alarming mourners betray the maze,
Only to themselves adultery remains praised.

If there was a moment of treason,
It fell on deaf ears of her season.
And to cheat one of one's own heart easing
Voids the calamity of reason.

The Dark Side of Our Mother ...I'm Sorry, But

So have I got your attention?
I definitely should mention
That our patience was running thin

From the world's blatant ignorance,
The wealthy's greedy arrogance,
And all those who point out sin.

None of us are worth more than her;
Some of us knew what had to occur.
Did you think mankind would win?

You may survive her first plague,
And still remain most vague,
But I'll promise a truth within.

Get ready for the storm
As it becomes the norm:
Virus mutation beyond our vaccines.

So, I'm sorry for this inconvenience,
I'm sorry that most are non-lenient,
But you were not even listening.

Got tired of your rat race,
Got tired of your grimace,
And her only choice ...retaliating.

"All Hail Gaia!" – So It Must Be!!!"

The Ebony Tides of Light

- (EVE) -
The luscious taunts of shadows at times seem dim,
Yet the darkness she brings is so subtle as it shimmers
Through her forest's foliage like candlelight in.
Her heavenly presence in opposite moods as a bringer
Of the nightfall for silence must
sometimes be heard within him.

- (DAYBREAK) -
At dawn's initiation, her induction brings new day,
And what follows is his manual labour to endure
For the writing on the wall is so vague in truth's way.
The truth of things is not one path but many for sure,
Yet if we follow only one road the
fallen will become as a lure.

- (NOON) -
When labours of time cease for
remission, her fruits are ample,
For no rest comes for the wicked of those who will tamper;
And to nullify the flowers and those who sample
Would destroy simplicity and intimacy
with no minutes to pamper.
The world would fall, giving no survival
mechanism nor children, for example.

THE FALLING SPIRAL OF GREED (Verse)

Needs may be wants, but wants are
complete opposites of necessity.
They will never be truth, unless for a
darkened heart, lost of faith
...And empty-bound into nothingness
...To cease existence
...To withdraw their choice for inclusion
...Into the UNITY of Continuity & Re-Creation.
Lessons / Lives to 100 cut short, and raped of a future,
To never have existed at all!
...For Immortality is in the Eternal Blood & NOT wealth
...And although my body must die, my
soul will always know health.

THE WHITE FIRE DRAGON: While You Were All Sleeping

With white fire in his eyes, he layeth ...watching ...waiting,
And the warmth he doth bring is of solace ...while gazing.
The apparent truth in his heart now racing ...enslaving
To break free of these chains now not ...of his making
For heart hath found a way to make ...all matters work.
Now this wonderful Puff will set forth life ...instead of hurt.

- Equality for all things willing it

The Vatican is free of my hate ...I do not forsake,
For Benedict came to me in daydream
and blessed me ...no ill fate.
He said unto me that my works ...be made true,
So, the books I have written are for ...and about all of you.
These books are made Fiction ...though
don't be fooled by their guise.
The morals in the Bible are throughout ...for they are wise
I have been summoned by The Ancestor
Guardians ...to write not for another church
Unless I could find a way to unite them
all ...and make it worth.

- While you were all sleeping,

...I saved the world
And so did you.
...I love you EGGS,
Bless you 1009-fold through.

...GOD Fave the Queen ...AMEN

These Scars of History

I once was innocent, and led to believe
That life would grant you wishes.
I believed in the benevolent, although deceived,
And outgrew those sordid britches.

I questioned all things, and got no answers
From the ones guiding me,
Rechose a path which doth bring life isn't cancer,
My path then rendered surely.

The burning of the history made it hard to learn,
But I knew it true deep within.
There is no hidden glory in lying or dis-concerned,
Ignorance the battlefield to trim.

They will knock you down and preach their ways,
But do not budge at all.
Take heed, friend: no frowns, teach the things you may,
Do this, and you may not fall.

Your life is up to you …So Mote It Be.

WHY?

Is this real, or is this just a bad dream?
I want to feel loved; I want to feel ...Ecstasy!
What's really happening? Why aren't you here?
I feel so empty now, so I just sit and stare:
Gazing, imagining, what ...how ...N' where.
What could've been? As I sit low in this chair.

How did it happen? Why did we part?
We were "perfect," and yet now ...Left in dark.
Will I ever see you again?
...I can only hope and wait for then.
...I can feel your touch ...I remember your smile,
So, I ask you 1 question ...Can you tell me ...Why?

(In Memory of My Dear Friend Kelly Kot ...R.I.P. Sweetheart)

The Calling
(A Poetic Prayer to the Angels)

Distant melodies of radiant softness
Falling upon my ears.
The sounds of nature filled with wellness
Calling out my fears.
Whispering an ancient magic,
Awakening my dreams,
Making me feel ye ole fantastic,
Even with melancholic themes.

There is a place inside ourselves
Where the bizarre is accepted,
Where love is kiss and tell,
And hate is not projected.
To be the one who grants us truth,
Coming home to kneel
Before the Aeons of the Light,
We open up the seals.

Temperance of our souls,
Deliverance of fulfillment,
Once again this ancient path
Pushes past deceiving temperament.
Never hang on to anger now;
Things will cling to you.
And time will heal ...Take a bow,
Let us all see this through.

Archangels of Love & Light,
Come to me please.
Manage my heart and cleanse my soul
So I can be at ease.
Let me see myself as is;
No ego is allowed.
And let me pray with your insight
To love myself more now.

❤ Blessed Be ❤

There is no end, for everything transforms, so

...TO BE CONTINUED

Milton Keynes UK
Ingram Content Group UK Ltd.
UKHW050220190124
436301UK00001B/2

9780228863564